Early one morning, Moana is
up by her little sister, S
It is Simea's birthd
looking for her prese

Moana tells Simea that they are going on a birthday treasure hunt!
Simea is excited, but she does not know what a treasure hunt is.

Moana says that it is a game where you find clues that lead you to treasure.
Today's treasure is Simea's birthday present.
The first clue is their mum's hair brush.

They find their mum
who says happy
birthday to Simea.
Sina had lost her brush
and is happy to have
it back.
Sina says she does not
know what the next clue is.

But Sina says that their dad forgot to take his lunch that day.
Simea thinks that must be a clue!
They will take their dad his lunch.
Their dad says happy birthday and thanks them for his lunch.

Chief Tui says it might not be a clue, but he does see something out of place.
Moana helps Simea spot the digging stick that is out of place.
Simea knows farmers use digging sticks in the fields.
They will take the stick to Kele.

Kele is glad to have his stick.
But he is not happy about the banana flowers that are in his way.

Could banana flowers be the next clue?
Kele tells them that banana flowers can be
used as a purple dye.

Simea knows that Moni uses dyes in his tapa. She rushes off to take them to him. Moana waves thank you to Kele.

Moni is glad someone has
picked the banana flowers
for him.
Simea looks at the table
for her next clue.
She sees a stone that looks
out of place.
Heihei likes it too.

Moana says it is a polishing stone.
Simea sees a drawing of Loto using a stone just like it.
They rush off to find Loto.

Simea tells Loto all about the treasure hunt.
Loto says she's done a great job.
Moana says the stone was the last clue and that
Simea's present is inside Loto's workshop.

Simea looks everywhere in the messy workshop.

At last, she finds her birthday present.
It is a tiny model of Moana's canoe!
It looks just like it, only cuter.

When Simea and Moana get home, they find all of their family and friends waiting for them.

They all wish Simea a happy birthday,
and they share a big feast.